D0091681

THIS BOOK CONTAINS:

ALIEN SLIME NINJAS
SUPERSECRET LEVEL-UP COMBOS
TWENTY-FOOT-TALL BUTT CHEEKS
NIGHT-VISION GOGGLES
BANANA BEASTS
MR. POOPSIE, THE BUTLER
AND
A MYSTERY!

Read the book. Find the clues. Level up.
Can you handle the awesomeness?
Well, what are you waiting for? **TURN THE PAGE!**

FUN FACT!

You can find all the Awesome Dog adventures in these books!

#1 *Awesome Dog 5000*

#2 *Awesome Dog 5000 vs. Mayor Bossypants*

#3 *Awesome Dog 5000 vs. the Kitty-Cat Cyber Squad*

AWESOME DOG 5000

JUSTIN DEAN

A Yearling Book

All rights reserved. Published in the United States by Yearling, an imprint of Random House Children's Books, a division of Penguin Random House LLC, New York. Originally published in hardcover in the United States by Random House Children's Books, a division of Penguin Random House LLC, New York, in 2019.

Yearling and the jumping horse design are registered trademarks of Penguin Random House LLC.

Visit us on the Web! rhcbooks.com

Educators and librarians, for a variety of teaching tools, visit us at RHTeachersLibrarians.com

The Library of Congress has cataloged the hardcover edition of this work as follows:
Names: Dean, Justin, author.
Title: Awesome Dog 5000 / Justin Dean.
Other titles: Awesome Dog five thousand
Description: First edition. | New York: Random House, [2019] |
Summary: When video game fanatic Marty, ten, arrives in a new town, his worst fear is being labeled a "dork" until the robotic dog he found catches the attention of a mad scientist.
Identifiers: LCCN 2018033232 | ISBN 978-0-525-64481-1 (trade) |
ISBN 978-0-525-64483-5 (lib. bdg.) | ISBN 978-0-525-64482-8 (ebook)
Subjects: | CYAC: Robots—Fiction. | Dogs—Fiction. | Adventure and adventurers—Fiction. | Schools—Fiction. | Popularity—Fiction. | Moving, Household—Fiction. | Science fiction.
Classification: LCC PZ7.1.D3985 Awe 2019 | DDC [Fic]—dc23

ISBN 978-0-525-64484-2 (pbk.)

Printed in the United States of America
10 9 8 7 6 5 4 3 2 1
First Yearling Edition 2021

This one is for Novak,
my most awesome-est best friend.

CHAPTER 1

Once Upon a Time in the Future

IT IS THE YEAR 3001, and the galaxy is at war. . . .

For over one hundred years, Earth has been under attack from alien slime ninjas. The bad guys are winning. They have captured the president of Earth and are holding her prisoner in the center of their moon maze base. Only one hero can free her. That hero is Sheriff Turbo-Karate. The mission to save the universe starts now!

THE MOON

Sheriff Turbo-Karate used his jet boots to fly through the maze. First, he turned left. Then he turned right. Then he turned left—

And was laser-sliced by a slime ninja's beam sword. It was a surprise attack! Sheriff Turbo-Karate took a direct hit through the chest. His cowboy hat popped off his head as he exploded into tiny specks of space dust!

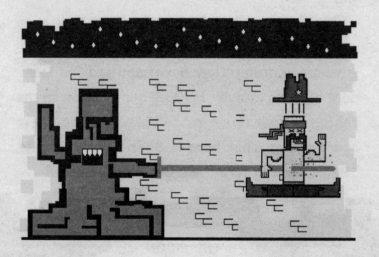

The mission to save the universe starts now: Sheriff Turbo-Karate used his jet boots to fly through the maze. First, he turned left. Then he turned right. Then he took a second right—

And accidentally stepped in chewing gum. It was another trap! His boot stuck to the floor as bombs showered over him. Sheriff Turbo-Karate was blasted into the stars.

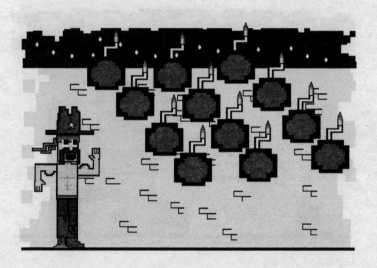

CONTINUE?

The mission to save the universe starts now: Sheriff Turbo-Karate used his jet boots to fly through the maze. First, he turned left. Then he turned right, then turned right again, jumped over the bubble gum, dodged the bomb shower—

And was zapped by a shrink ray. The alien slime ninjas caught him and held him prisoner in a stinky shoebox for the rest of his life.

The mission to save the universe starts now: Sheriff Turbo-Karate used his jet boots to fly through the maze. First, he—

PAUSE

Marty Fontana leaned back in his seat and set aside his video game, *Sheriff Turbo-Karate*. Marty was ten years old, had spiky yellow hair, and always wore red high-top sneakers. He was bored after trying to beat the moon maze level on his video game so many times. Marty had been riding in a moving van with his mom for hours. They were driving to his new house. Marty's mom had recently been hired to start a different job—

Okay. Wait. Before we get too far ahead, there should be a warning to the reader.

BOOK WARNING! BOOK WARNING! BOOK WARNING!

If you expected some super-cool, action-packed start with rocket jets and an evil dude and a daring rescue mission, this story isn't for you.* Our apologies if you were confused. Even though the title of the book is *Awesome Dog 5000*, this story is actually about a regular kid who moves into a boring old house and starts going to a new school.

And really, that's about it.

---

* All the action-packed stuff with rocket jets, an evil dude, and a daring rescue mission starts later, like around chapter 11.

CHAPTER 2

Where the Story Really Starts

MARTY AND HIS MOM arrived at their new house, but it didn't feel very new. Everything was covered in dust, like no one had been there for decades. The living room had towers of cardboard boxes filled with old science books, faded blueprints, and rusted tools.

"Who left all this stuff here?" Marty asked his mom.

"The last owner," she said. "I heard he was some fancy-electric-toothbrush inventor. They said he created some super-toothbrush that brushed your hair and your teeth at the same time."

A painting of the inventor hung above the fireplace. He was an old man with messy gray hair and a silly mustache. He was holding an electric tooth-brush. It was strange. The *whole house* was strange.

This place didn't feel like home to Marty. It made him miss his old house and his old friends. At his last school, Marty had a ton of friends, but he didn't know anyone in this new town. It all made him worry about starting fifth grade somewhere different. He asked, "Mom, what if the kids here don't like me?"

"Of course they will," she said. "What's not to like? You're a cool dude who likes pizza and video games."

Marty didn't just like video games. He loooooooved video games. His favorite video game was, obviously, *Sheriff Turbo-Karate*. It had sweet old-school graphics, a great story, and up to four-player co-op. Plus, you could do secret combo attacks like:

ROCKET CHOPS

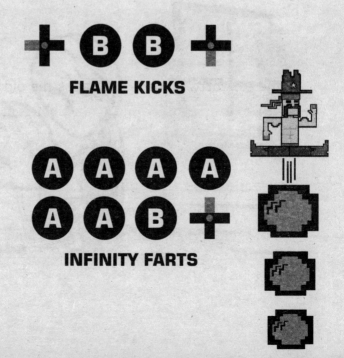

FLAME KICKS

INFINITY FARTS

That last combo Marty had found by accident. It didn't actually hurt enemies, but it always made Marty laugh to watch the sheriff toot around the screen. Unfortunately, Marty wasn't in a laughing mood today.

Marty's mom saw her son's frown. She could tell he was still nervous about school. She knelt down next to him and very sweetly asked, "Can I give you some advice, Marty?"

Marty nodded. His mom always knew how to help.

"Don't overthink it. Just be yourself," she said. Marty's mom gave him a big hug. It made him feel a lot better. Then she told him, "I mean, what's the worst that could happen?"

Marty thought of one very, very bad thing that could happen.

CHAPTER 3

The Not-to-Do List

THERE IS ONE THING every kid fears when starting at a new school. It's being called the dreaded "d" word. And, no, it's not "dragonslayer," or "dolphin trainer," or even "dolly dressmaker."

The "d" word is "dork."

Everyone knows that if you're called a dork— even once—you'll be a dork forever. You'll be known as a dork in elementary school, in middle

school, in high school, and even when you're old. Your grandkids will call you Grandpappy Dork and then point and laugh.

Being a dork also means it is impossible to ever make any friends. No one dares hang out with someone marked by the letter "d." Dorkiness is like having the flu. Just being near a dork can spread the dorkiness and make people think you're one as well. The "d" word is a lonely, friendless curse, and Marty refused to let it happen to him.

The morning of Marty's first day of school, he got his backpack and school supplies ready. He sat down at his desk and brainstormed all the things that made someone a dork. He wrote a checklist of everything not to do.

It was three simple rules.

3 THINGS <u>NOT</u> TO DO ON MY FIRST DAY

1. DO <u>NOT</u> DO ANYTHING WEIRD

2. DO <u>NOT</u> DO ANYTHING EMBARRASSING

3. DO <u>NOT</u> DO ANYTHING UNCOOL!!!

If Marty followed these rules, he would be dork-proof. He would make friends, be super cool, and never be made fun of by his grandkids. It was all Marty wanted.

Marty changed into his favorite Sheriff Turbo-Karate T-shirt and strapped on his backpack. He started his first day at his new school, Nikola Tesla Elementary.

And it went terribly.

CHAPTER 4

First Day, Worst Day

THE SCHOOL BELL RANG, and class began. Marty's teacher, Mrs. Taylor, called him to the front of the classroom and asked him to introduce himself to the other students. Marty was incredibly nervous. His stomach was doing flips, and his hands were sweaty. Instead of saying "Hi, my name is Marty Fontana," he accidentally mixed up his words and said "Hi, my name is Farty Montana."

The entire class burst into laughter and pointed at him for saying "Farty." There went rule number one:

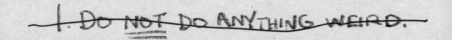

1. Do not do anything weird.

In gym class, they played basketball. It was the fifth graders versus the sixth graders. Marty was excited. Basketball was his favorite sport, and he was pretty good at it. During the game, he scored a few baskets, blocked some shots, and even stole a pass from the other team.

There was less than a minute left on the clock, and the score was tied: 30–30. The fifth graders had the ball and a chance to win it all.

Marty ran downcourt, and a teammate threw him the ball. All the sixth graders immediately swarmed Marty. He couldn't get a clear shot or even make a pass. He'd have to use his b-ball skills to get to the basket before time ran out.

Marty faked right but ran left. He did a quick spin, circled back, dribbled behind his legs, and spun two more times. He broke past the defenders and aimed for the basket. Marty took the shot.

The basketball soared high into the air and hit the backboard. It dropped to the rim and wobbled on the edge. Then . . . tipped in with a swoosh.

The buzzer sounded. The game was over, and Marty had made the basket!

"YES!" Marty exclaimed. He jumped up into the air with a flying fist pump. He stuck his butt out and did a silly booty-shake dance to celebrate. All his teammates frowned at him like he was a wiggle-maniac with ants in the pants.

From across the court, a sixth grader yelled out to Marty, "Thanks for the help, new kid!" Then all the sixth graders high-fived each other.

The help? Marty thought. He gave a confused look at the scoreboard.

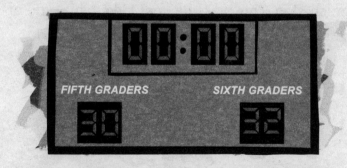

In the final seconds of the game, Marty had done so many spins and twists that he'd gotten turned around and had shot at the wrong basket. Marty hadn't just won the game for the other team—he'd danced around like an idiot afterward, too.

Bye-bye, rule number two:

2. Do not do anything embarrassing.

Next was lunch in the cafeteria. The lunch lady served Marty two scoops of gray slop with a side of greenish-brown goop. It smelled like food, but it definitely didn't look like it. Marty took his tray of "food" and walked up to a table of kids. There was one empty seat left.

"Can I sit here?" Marty asked.

All the kids gave disgusted looks to Marty's lunch slop. This was the cool kids' table, and at this school, cool kids never ate cafeteria food.

They only ate sack lunches. Marty blew it.

That was his third strike:

3. ~~Do NOT Do ANYTHING UNCOOL!!!~~

"This new kid eats puke food!" said a boy wearing sunglasses. His name was Shades. Shades was the leader of the cool kids. He was so cool that he always wore sunglasses. He even wore them when he slept, so he would look cool in his dreams.

Shades said to Marty, "You don't belong at this table. Get outta here, dork!"

A hush fell over the entire cafeteria. If you were watching a movie, this would be the part where the music goes:

DUN! DUN! DUUUUU-UUUUUU-UUUUUN!

Marty had been called the dreaded "d" word, and the whole school had heard it.

CHAPTER 5

"D"-feated

EVERY EYE in the cafeteria was focused on Marty. The other students were curious to see how the new kid would react to being branded a dork. Marty didn't cry or yell out in anger. He just wanted to hide.

He searched the cafeteria for an open seat. He rushed from table to table but was denied every time. It was a series of "nope," "no way," "absolutely not," and "AAAAAAH! Get away from us! You're cursed!" Everyone treated Marty like he was a dork zombie looking for brains. No one wanted to risk his dorkiness spreading to their table.

After repeatedly being rejected, Marty finally gave up and stood by the trash can to eat his "food." He had never felt so alone in his whole life. Marty wanted so badly to go back to his old home with his old friends, and never to come to this school again.

Just then a kid with square glasses and messy brown hair walked up. "Hey! You're that new student!" he said.

Marty nodded. "Yeah. I'm the dorky new kid."

"You seem pretty cool to me," the boy said. "You told that hilarious joke in class about being named Farty. And you were awesome in gym! I passed you the ball for the last shot. You've got some amazing basketball skills. I've never seen a fifth grader dribble between his legs before."

Marty was confused. He saw all the things he'd
done earlier as mistakes, but this kid thought
they were something to be proud of.

"If you're not doing anything, you want to join
a school club?" asked the boy in the glasses. "It's a
lot of fun, and we have our daily meetings during
lunch."

Marty wanted to jump up and down.

YES! PLEASE! HOLY MOON CHEESE ON A CRACKER! WHEW, BABY! WHERE DO I SIGN UP FOR THIS CLUB? I WILL DO ANYTHING TO SIT AT A TABLE AND NOT BE THE DORK HANGING OUT BY THE TRASH CAN!

That was what he wanted to say. Instead, he was so shocked that all that came out of his mouth was "Uh . . . yup."

Marty followed the boy in glasses across the cafeteria—all the way across the cafeteria. They walked and walked and walked to the farthest corner on the opposite side of the room. The journey was so long that Marty worried his milk would spoil into moldy yogurt.

The boys finally arrived at a wobbly old table with only three legs. There wasn't any student meeting taking place. It was just a girl with swooshy black hair with a purple streak. A skateboard sat across her lap, and she was eating from a tray of cafeteria food.

"I, uh, thought you said this was a club?" Marty asked.

"It is," the boy in glasses said. He held his arms out wide, smiled big, and announced, "Welcome to the Zeroes Club!"

CHAPTER 6

The Zeroes Club

EACH CAFETERIA TABLE at Nikola Tesla Elementary had a number painted on it. There were twenty tables in total.

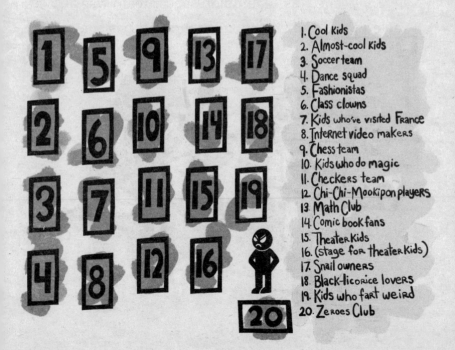

1. Cool Kids
2. Almost-cool kids
3. Soccer team
4. Dance squad
5. Fashionistas
6. Class clowns
7. Kids who've visited France
8. Internet video makers
9. Chess team
10. Kids who do magic
11. Checkers team
12. Chi-Chi-Mookipon players
13. Math Club
14. Comic book fans
15. Theater kids
16. (stage for theater kids)
17. Snail owners
18. Black-licorice lovers
19. Kids who fart weird
20. Zeroes Club

Table #1 was considered the best because it was farthest from the watchful eyes of the on-duty teacher. The students who sat at table #1 could break school rules without being caught. They used their cell phones, traded homework answers, and drank soda. This, of course, was the cool kids' table, where Shades and his friends ate their sack lunches.

At this school, you could tell how popular a group of friends were by where they sat. The lower the number, the cooler they were. So, for example, the state-champion soccer team was at table #3. All the creepy kids who had pet snails were stuck at #17.

Marty had been invited to sit at table #20, the absolute lowest-ranked table in the cafeteria. It was specially reserved for the dorkiest of dorks and total outcasts. "The dorkiest of dorks and total outcasts" isn't a very catchy name for a group, so instead they called themselves the Zeroes Club. This was because the table's painted #20 had worn off to a single faded 0.

The Zeroes Club members were the boy in glasses, the girl with the swooshy hair, and now Marty—if he accepted the invitation.

"I'm Ralph and this is Skyler," said the boy to Marty. "So do you want to join our club?"

Marty was about to answer, when Skyler pointed at his shirt. "Hey! You play *Sheriff Turbo-Karate?!* Oh. You are going to fit right in with us!"

She showed Marty her skateboard. The bottom was covered in *Sheriff Turbo-Karate* stickers.

"Fun fact! *Sheriff Turbo-Karate* is the Zeroes Club's all-time favorite video game!" said Ralph.

This was how Marty met Ralph Rogers and Skyler Kwon.

CHAPTER 7

The Kwon Family Tree

EVER SINCE KINDERGARTEN, Skyler Kwon had never quite fit in at school. She had her own unique style the other kids thought was strange. Her clothes, her hair, and even the music she liked confused most people. (Ever heard of the Swedish all-girl metal band Samürai Mermaid?) Skyler didn't care about being popular or following new trends. That's why the cool kids had labeled her a weirdo and banished her to table #20.

But Skyler was proud of being different.

There was a boldness to everything she did. Whether dyeing her hair punk-rock purple or sliding handrails on her skateboard, Skyler was fearless.

She got her confident spirit from her parents. Her mom was a race car driver, and her dad was

SKYLER'S BEDROOM

METAL BAND POSTER

SAMURAI

MERMAID

COOL DRAWINGS

BOOK REPORT ON AMELIA EARHART

SKATEBOARD (OBVIOUSLY)

ROCK JAMS

FUNSTATION GAME SYSTEM

a skydiving teacher. They had taught her from a young age always to be brave, but sometimes she had a little too much courage. When Skyler was a baby, she would ramp her stroller off the roof and use her diaper to parachute into the front yard.*

Skyler came from a long line of daredevils. Her grandfather once roller-skated down an erupting volcano, her aunts

were chainsaw jugglers, and her cousin was a shark dentist. Her family had always been daring, going back to the Ice Age. The original Kwon had discovered fire just so he could jump over it with his caveman motorcycle.

But this isn't a boring history book, so let's fast-forward a million years . . . skipping past the pyramids, the Vikings, and disco dancing to the modern day, when Ralph Rogers is the weirdest kid in fifth grade.

---

* Book safety disclaimer: This dangerous trick should only be attempted by professionally trained stunt babies.

CHAPTER 8

Fun Facts About Ralph

RALPH ROGERS is a great kid but a bit of an oddball. For example, Ralph spent last summer memorizing ninety-seven books in the library. Now he has too many facts floating around in his head, and they sometimes spill out.

Like you'll be watching a movie with Ralph and you'll try to share your popcorn and he'll say, "Fun fact! Aztec kings in Mexico used popcorn to decorate their crowns."

And then you miss that cool action scene with the helicopter explosion because Ralph was talking about a hat. Anyway, here are the top five fun facts about Ralph:

FUN FACT #5: Ralph taught a scorpion how to do a backflip.

FUN FACT #4: Ralph can play exactly one song on the keytar. It's like a guitar, but it's a keyboard.

FUN FACT #3: Ralph has a collection of rocks that look like Abraham Lincoln.

FUN FACT #2: Ralph was stung in the head by a backflipping scorpion.

FUN FACT #1: Ralph's all-time favorite video game is *Sheriff Turbo-Karate.* He even dressed up as the video game hero last Halloween.

And fun fact number one brings us right back to the cafeteria, where Skyler noticed Marty's *Sheriff Turbo-Karate* shirt and Ralph said, "Fun fact! *Sheriff Turbo-Karate* is the Zeroes Club's all-time favorite game!"

"Mine too," said Marty. "But I can't get through the moon maze."

"Us either," said Ralph.

"Maybe if we teamed up in three-player co-op mode, we could figure it out together," said Skyler.

And just like that, a dork did the impossible. Marty made some friends.

CHAPTER 9

Game Time

AFTER SCHOOL, Ralph and Skyler got their game systems and met up with Marty at his house. Marty introduced his mom to his new friends. Mrs. Fontana suggested the kids hang out in the living room while she unpacked the last of the moving boxes in Marty's bedroom.

The kids pulled up some cardboard boxes for seats and were ready to play their favorite video game, *Sparkle Rainbow Tea Party Adventure*. It was a cute game where you sit at a tea party and you talk about nice things like sweet kittens, and pretty flowers, and how to be polite—

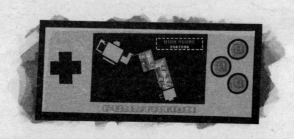

Just kidding. They played . . .

The kids linked their video games to three-player co-op mode and selected their sheriffs' hats. They all picked their favorite colors: Marty was red, Ralph was blue, and Skyler was purple (just like the streak in her hair). They hit start and set off into the moon maze. Their sheriffs made left and right turns. They jetted through star caves and space tunnels. They worked together avoiding traps and the alien slime army. Their teamwork paid off, and they reached the center of the maze. The sheriffs stood in front of a giant golden door.

"Fun fact!" said Ralph. "You can win a gold medal for trampoline jumping in the Olympics."

That fact didn't have anything to do with the game, but Ralph said it anyway because, well, that's Ralph.

The golden door swung open to reveal a giant throne room. Inside, the president of Earth was being held prisoner. She was locked in a cage hanging from the ceiling. She pleaded, "Help me, Sheriffs! You're my only hope!"

Getting the cage's key wasn't going to be easy. It hung around the neck of the Blob King. The king was enormous. His eyes were bright red, his

teeth were razor sharp, and his life meter was fifty hearts strong. This was the final boss.

The battle began, and Marty, Ralph, and Skyler furiously mashed buttons. They all karate-chopped the Blob King, but nothing damaged the king's health.

"Even against all three of us, he's too strong!" said Skyler.

"There must be a secret way to beat him," said Ralph.

That gave Marty the perfect idea. He told Skyler and Ralph his secret combo moves. They unlocked the power attacks: rocket chops, flying knee slams, and flame kicks. But they didn't work, either. The king was still at full health.

"Your combos are lame!" said the Blob King. He did a super slap, and the sheriffs' health dropped to one heart each.

"If we're hit again, it's game over," said Ralph. "Marty, do you know any more secret moves?"

"I only know one more combo, but it's not an attack move," said Marty.

"It doesn't matter what the move is," Skyler said. "We have to try it!"

Marty entered into his controller A, A, A, A, A, A, B, UP. It was the "infinity farts" combo.

Instantly, his sheriff jumped around and farted up the throne room. Stinky brown gas filled the screen. The king gagged from the smell. "YUCK! YOUR SECRET COMBO STINKS!"

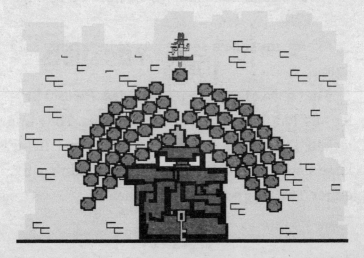

The king was blinded by the brown gas, but his health remained full.

"It isn't working. He still isn't losing any hearts," said Marty.

"No. Keep it up!" said Skyler. "It's distracting him. I think I can grab the key!"

Marty's red sheriff's toots gave Skyler cover. She sneaked through the thick gas and swiped the key from around the king's neck.

"Quick! I'll give you a boost, Skyler!" said Ralph. He moved his sheriff underneath the cage. Skyler did a running jump, sprang off the top of the blue sheriff's head, and then flipped up through the air. She inserted the key, opened the cage, and saved Earth's president. On their screens, a graphic popped up:

All three kids leapt from their seats. Ralph yelled out, "We beat it! I can't believe we actually saved the universe! That cheat code was amazing, Marty!"

"Thanks," said Marty. "Fast thinking on grabbing the key, Skyler!"

"I couldn't have done it without the jump assist from Ralph!" said Skyler.

"Zeroes Club in the house! Woop-woop!" said Ralph.

The kids were so fired up, they started jumping up and down. They bounced around so much that it shook the wooden floorboards. The vibrations knocked over a stack of dusty boxes in the living room corner.

"Hey, what is that?" asked Ralph. He pointed to a box that had fallen over.

"It's just old junk that a weird toothbrush inventor left behind when he moved out," said Marty.

"That's definitely not junk," said Skyler. "I think that inventor made something a little bit cooler than a toothbrush."

Inside one of the tipped-over boxes was a small robot dog.

CHAPTER 10

The A.W.S.M. 5000

THE KIDS TOOK the robot dog out of the box and set him on his feet. He looked like a beagle made of battleship metal. He was by far the most amazing thing they ever had seen in their entire ten-year-old lives. And Ralph had once seen an internet video of a panda jumping on a pogo stick.

Marty pressed the small power button on the back of the dog's collar. . . .

Nothing happened. The robot dog stood motionless.

"I think he needs batteries," said Ralph. "There's a slot on the dog's belly marked 'Batteries go here.'"

The kids couldn't find batteries in any of the moving boxes, so Marty swiped two AA batteries from the TV remote. They inserted them into the dog's battery slot and flipped the power switch. The hum of a motor buzzed inside the dog's chest. His eyes lit up. He was powered on but still didn't move.

"Is he supposed to do something?" asked Skyler. She knocked on the dog's head to wake up his brain. "Hello? Is anyone home in there?"

Marty checked the robot dog's cardboard box.

It was empty. There were no instructions. There was no user guide. The kids would have to figure out how to use the dog on their own.

"It's a robot dog. So maybe it's programmed with some dog tricks," Ralph said.

Skyler tried a dog command. "Sit!"

The robot dog sat. The kids were shocked.

"Roll over!" said Ralph.

The robot dog rolled over.

"Speak!" said Marty.

A loud robot voice boomed from a speaker on the dog's collar. "BARK. BARK. I AM THE A.W.S.M. THE AUTOWORK AND SERVICE MACHINE 5000 MODEL!"

"That name is way too long to remember," said Ralph. "We should rename him something shorter, like Spot or Phillip, or—I got it! Ralph Junior."

"We're not calling him Ralph Junior. That's silly," said Skyler. "He needs a cool name, like Bark-o-saurus Rex!"

Marty wasn't sure about either of those names. He looked back at the robot dog's box. Letters and numbers were written across the side. Marty sounded out the letters. "A-W-S-M 5000. Ay-was-em 5000 . . . Ahs-mee 5000. Aws-em?"

Then he got it.

"Awesome! A.W.S.M. stands for 'awesome'! Let's call him Awesome Dog 5000!"

The robot dog spoke. "BARK. BARK. I AM AWE-SOME DOG 5000!"

"Nice to meet you, Awesome Dog. I'm Marty, and these are my friends Ralph and Skyler."

"BARK. BARK. NICE TO MEET YOU. BARK. BARK. CAN WE GO FOR A WALK?" asked Awesome Dog.

A leash unspooled from the dog's collar. Marty opened the front door and picked up the leash. He said, "Sure, let's go for a wa—"

But before Marty could finish his sentence, Awesome Dog's paws instantly switched into four rocket jets. He blasted off, yanking Marty with him. They flew straight through the doorway at three hundred miles per hour.

Skyler and Ralph chased after them out to the front yard, but Awesome Dog jetted up into the sky. Marty and the dog were gone.

From inside the house, Ralph and Skyler heard Marty's mom yell, "HEY! WHY IS MY TV REMOTE NOT WORKING?!"

CHAPTER 11

Finally, It's the Part of the Story with the Rocket Jets, an Evil Dude, and a Rescue Mission (Took Long Enough, Sheesh!)

AWESOME DOG ROCKETED through the clouds, pulling Marty behind him. Marty held tight to the leash as they soared twenty thousand feet above the ground. They were so high up that Marty could see the entire town. All the people looked like tiny bugs, and the cars like toys.

Marty yelled, "Put me down, Awesome Dog!"

"BARK. BARK. GOING DOWN, MARTY!" the dog said.

Awesome Dog took a nosedive toward a giant mansion below. This wasn't what Marty meant at all.

They smashed through the mansion's roof and flew down a grand hallway. Dozens of doors whooshed by Marty in a blur. "Get us out of here!" screamed Marty.

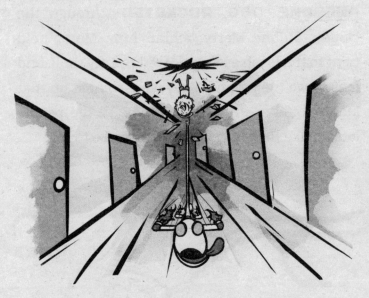

"BARK. BARK. GETTING OUT OF HALLWAY," said Awesome Dog.

Awesome Dog sped up his rockets. He rammed

through a wall and into the mansion's kitchen. They flew past a refrigerator and soared over the oven. They plowed through a stack of plastic cups and a punch bowl. They were splashed with red juice and headed toward a huge chocolate cake in the middle of the room.

"LOOK OUT!" yelled Marty.

Awesome Dog cut a quick turn and narrowly missed the cake, but Marty was jerked into it face-first. He smashed through the cake in an explosion of brown frosting.

It didn't stop Awesome Dog. He crashed into another room.

The room was filled with hundreds and hundreds of floating balloons. This mansion was so fancy it didn't just have a ballroom. It had a ball-*oon* room.

Awesome Dog weaved between balloons like he was zipping along a winding road. As Marty whipped left and right, a big smile broke over his face. Jet flying wasn't too scary after you were used to it. Marty was having fun. "Go faster, Awesome Dog!" yelled Marty.

Awesome Dog tilted his rocket paws down and

flew up through the ceiling. They jetted away as Marty looked back at the destroyed mansion. A butler and an angry-looking bald man were in the front yard. Marty yelled an apology. "Sorry about trashing your mansion, bald dude! This dog is crazy!"

The bald man shouted something, but Marty was too high up to hear what he said. Marty flew back home without knowing that the mansion was owned by a very bad guy. This very bad guy now wanted revenge on a little boy and his robot dog.

CHAPTER 12

Dr. Crazybrains's Birthday Party

DR. CRAZYBRAINS was a mad scientist with a big, shiny bald head and a little beard on his chin. He was one of the smartest people in the world but only used his genius for evil.

Dr. Crazybrains invented evil potions and sold them to other supervillains. He kept thousands of

bottles on his giant potion wall: formulas to turn people into lobsters, a potion that made people stink like dirty socks, warp potions, silly-mustache potions, and any other potion imaginable.

Every potion was custom-made, and the doctor kept the recipes a secret. None of the potion bottles listed the ingredients or even had words. Instead, they were labeled with a simple picture. This kept people from stealing his formulas. The doctor was the only one who knew each potion's effects, and you'd have to buy them to find out what they did.

Now, you're probably saying to yourself: "Hey, wait a second, Book! What does any of this have to do with the story?" Well, just keep reading. You'll find out soon enough—and quit being so impatient. It's rude.

Selling potions made Dr. Crazybrains rich. So rich, in fact, that he lived in a giant mansion with a secret underground lab. This was the same giant mansion Marty and Awesome Dog crashed into.

AZYBRAINS'S MANSION

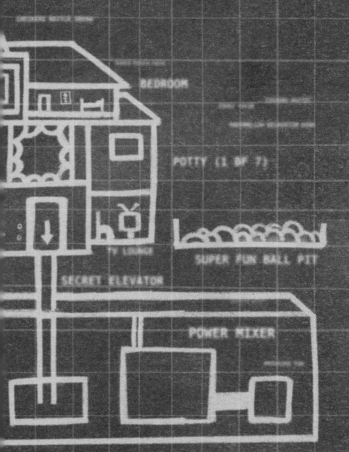

BEDROOM

POTTY (1 OF 7)

SUPER FUN BALL PIT

TV LOUNGE

SECRET ELEVATOR

POWER MIXER

Let's rewind the story back a few weeks earlier:

Dr. Crazybrains planned on throwing himself a big fiftieth-birthday party. He ordered a giant birthday cake, a huge bowl of punch, and seven hundred balloons for his ball-oon room. He sent invitations out to all his supervillain friends. Everything was ready for the celebration.

On the day of his party, Dr. Crazybrains was in his underground lab experimenting on his newest evil potion. He named it Freaky Fruit Juice. The potion transformed fruit into creepy-crawly little monsters with sharp fangs. The doctor was creating a bunch of banana beasts to give out as party favors, but an hour before his guests were to arrive, there was a loud crash upstairs.

He called for his butler. "That sounded like a small robotic dog just crashed through my cake. Let's go check it out, Mr. Poopsie!"

His butler's real name was Bob Smith, but Dr. Crazybrains was so evil he called his butler Mr. Poopsie.

The doctor and his butler found a mess in the mansion's kitchen. There was punch spilled across the tile floor, and his birthday cake was destroyed. He followed the trail of brown frosting to his ball-oon room. He saw a giant hole blasted through the ceiling. All his balloons were floating away. The doctor and his butler quickly ran out to the front yard to catch a look at what had caused the damage.

Dr. Crazybrains saw Marty and Awesome Dog flying away. He heard Marty yell, "Sorry about trashing your mansion, bald dude!"

The doctor was furious. He screamed out, "YOU RUINED MY BIRTHDAY PARTY! I'LL GET MY REVENGE ON YOU!"

But Marty was too high to hear him.

"How do you propose we catch the vandals,

sir?" asked Mr. Poopsie. "They've escaped into the sky."

"I'll use one of my potions," said Dr. Crazy-brains.

He pulled out a potion bottle. Its label had a shoe with blurry dash lines. This was Flash Splash. For exactly five minutes, it made you run faster than a cheetah riding a roller coaster. The doctor gulped it down and bolted out the door—

FOUR MINUTES . . .

AND . . .

FIFTY-NINE
SECONDS LATER.

The doctor raced across town following the trail of chocolate cake frosting. It led Dr. Crazybrains to an old house that had belonged to a toothbrush inventor he once knew.

The doctor found a hiding spot across the street. From behind a tree, he watched as Awesome Dog, Ralph, Skyler, and Marty played in the front yard.

Now Dr. Crazybrains knew exactly what he was up against.

CHAPTER 13

Dog Tricks

WHEN MARTY RETURNED HOME, the first thing he did was change out of his dirty clothes. The second thing he did was tell Ralph and Skyler about his mansion adventure.

"You flew through the clouds, then crashed into a mansion?! This dog is awesome! I want to take him for a walk," said Skyler.

"No, no, no. We have to be careful when playing with Awesome Dog," warned Marty. "It can be very dangerous. I've got cake in my underwear to prove it."

"Why don't we just play fetch?" suggested Ralph. "Nothing bad can happen with a dog running after a stick."

Marty picked up a stick and threw it across the yard.

Awesome Dog watched the stick land in the grass. He stared at it for a moment, then looked back to Marty.

"Wow," Skyler said in a bored tone. "This is sooooo much more fun than sky surfing."

Ralph pointed at the stick and said, "Get the stick, Awesome Dog!"

"GET THAT STICK!" commanded Marty.

"BARK. BARK. ACTIVATE MEGA-CANNON!" said Awesome Dog.

Suddenly, a giant bazooka extended out from Awesome Dog's back. The mega-cannon took aim and fired.

The stick erupted in a massive explosion. The blast knocked all three kids back ten feet. A plume of fire scorched the grass. A mushroom cloud of black smoke rose high into the sky.

Skyler laughed. "Awesome Dog really *got* that stick!"

Dr. Crazybrains was spying on the kids from behind a tree. His eyes went wide, and his jaw dropped when he saw the explosion. He didn't dare mess with Marty now. The boy was protected by a robot dog with a mega-cannon. Instead, the doctor did what all evil bad guys do when faced with a challenge: he ran away like a scaredy-cat.

The doctor needed to think up the perfect evil revenge plan.

CHAPTER 14

The Perfect Evil Revenge Plan

DR. CRAZYBRAINS CALLED his supervillain friends to let them know his birthday party was canceled. He set his monster-fruit experiment aside and focused his full attention on his revenge against Marty. He stayed up all night brainstorming evil ideas and scribbling them out on his chalkboard. The next morning, he revealed his perfect evil revenge plan to Mr. Poopsie.

"If this dog is always guarding those kids," said Dr. Crazybrains, "where is the one place they won't be together?"

"China," said Mr. Poopsie.

"NO!" screeched Dr. Crazybrains. "Not China! SCHOOL! SCHOOL! School is where they won't be together! GOSH, YOU ARE SUCH A NINCOM-POOPSIE!"

Then the doctor laid out his plan. "First," he said, "I sneak into school. This is the one place the robot dog won't be, because dogs aren't allowed in school. Neither are robots.

"Second: I go to the cafeteria disguised as a lunch lady and wait for the spiky-haired kid to get in line. I then pour my Igloo-Goo Potion into his food.

"Third: The boy eats the potion, and it turns him into an ice statue. Fourth: I bring the frozen kid back to my lab. Fifth: I play the video game *Sparkle Rainbow Tea Party Adventure*. Sixth: I explain my amazing backstory of how I became a supervillain. Seventh: I use my evilest potion on the boy and get my revenge."

Dr. Crazybrains paused to take a breath. "And eighth: I call my mommy to see if she's proud of me."

Dr. Crazybrains threw his head back and gave a loud evil laugh. "Mwa-ha-ha-ha-ha-ha-ha!"

Mr. Poopsie held up a finger and timidly asked, "Er, beg your pardon for interrupting your evil laughing, but why is playing *Sparkle Rainbow Tea Party Adventure* part of the revenge plan?"

Dr. Crazybrains screamed, "BECAUSE IT'S MY FAVORITE VIDEO GAME!" The doctor took a deep breath and calmed down. He continued. "Also, it takes about twenty minutes for the Igloo-Goo to wear off, and I get bored waiting."

The doctor spent the weekend crafting his disguise and brewing a fresh batch of the freeze potion. First thing Monday morning, he set out for Nikola Tesla Elementary School. Evil revenge was coming for Marty, and it looked like a fifty-year-old bald dude in a lunch lady costume.

CHAPTER 15

(Mis)Step #3

DR. CRAZYBRAINS COMPLETED the first two steps of his perfect evil revenge plan. He had sneaked into the elementary school disguised as one of the lunch ladies. Once Marty got into the cafeteria line, Dr. Crazybrains would get . . .

HIS EVIL REVENGE!

But Marty never showed up. None of the students did.

Unfortunately, Dr. Crazybrains forgot to check the calendar before starting his evil revenge plan. Monday was a school holiday.

The doctor returned the very next day. Tuesday would be the day Dr. Crazybrains would get . . .

HIS EVIL REVENGE!

But Marty had a dentist appointment in the morning and missed lunch.

So Dr. Crazybrains came back on Wednesday to get . . .

HIS EVIL REVE—

Nope. Didn't happen that day, either. Marty's class took a field trip to the planetarium.

On Thursday, Dr. Crazybrains forgot to set his alarm clock. He accidentally overslept in the morning and didn't get to the cafeteria in time for lunch. The principal was very upset at the new employee, "Dr. Lunch Lady," for being late to work.

Friday, Marty's class had a pizza party on the playground because everyone got an A on the spelling test. This is how you spell the doctor's mood when he found out: P-O-U-T-Y-P-A-N-T-S.

Waiting a whole week to get his revenge made the doctor one thousand times angrier than he was before. He immediately rushed back to his mansion to release his evil frustration. He punched his collection of beanbag chairs. He kicked the fluffy white walls of his marshmallow room. Then he took a relaxing swim through his giant super-fun ball pit.

The next Monday morning, Mr. Poopsie double-checked that it wasn't a school holiday, woke up Dr. Crazybrains extra early for work, and freshly shampooed his lunch-lady wig. He wanted to make sure the doctor had a perfect evil revenge day. The butler even made Dr. Crazybrains his favorite breakfast: blueberry waffles with a glass of hand-squeezed orange juice.

"Thank you so much," said Dr. Crazybrains with a smile. "This is just what I needed."

He then threw the table across the kitchen. The waffles went flying, and the plate smashed into pieces.

Dr. Crazybrains screamed, "JUST WHAT I NEEDED TO GET ME IN THE MOOD FOR REVENGE!!!"

CHAPTER 16

No More Mr. Ice Guy

DR. CRAZYBRAINS was back in the cafeteria disguised as a lunch lady when he saw Marty, Ralph, and Skyler get in line for lunch. It was finally time for step three. The doctor secretly put a dose of Igloo-Goo into a scoop of lunch slop. He served it to Marty.

"Enjoy your lunch and have an ice day—

I mean, have a nice day!" said Dr. Crazybrains in a silly lunch-lady voice.

"Uh, thanks. You too," said Marty.

At first the kids thought it was weird that their new lunch lady had a beard, wore a wig, kept telling everyone how cool *Sparkle Rainbow Tea Party Adventure* was, and actually looked nothing like a lunch lady at all, but they were too polite to say anything.

The kids took their lunch slop and sat at table 0. Marty had a bite of his "food" and said to his friends, "Hey, when we get home today, what new twicks should we try wiff Awthum Dog?" Marty was trying to say "What new tricks should we try with Awesome Dog?" but his tongue was suddenly cold and numb.

Skyler pointed. "Whoa! Marty, your tongue! It's turned blue."

"Fun fact! A blue whale's tongue weighs as much as an elephant," said Ralph.

Marty ran to the window and stuck his tongue out at his reflection. It was not only blue—it was frozen solid.

Dr. Crazybrains saw the potion taking effect. He jumped onto a table and ripped off his disguise. "Ahha! Step three of my perfect evil revenge plan is finally complete! I tricked you into eating a freeze potion because you crashed my birthday party!"

"Happy birthday, Ms. Lunch Lady!" said Ralph. He really didn't know what was going on, but he always tried to be nice.

Marty remembered seeing the doctor before. Marty said with a numb tongue, "Oh no! Ith the angry bald guy from the manthion! I'm tho thorry! It wath an athident, mither."

Ralph and Skyler looked confused, but the

doctor knew what Marty was trying to say, and it threw him into a rage.

"How dare you call me 'mister'! I am a doctor! Dr. Crazybrains!" He hopped off the table and said, "And now you're coming with me!"

The doctor was hit in the back of the head with a glop of cafeteria food. He looked over his shoulder and saw that Skyler was the one who'd thrown it.

"You leave our friend alone! Or else!" ordered Skyler.

"Or else what?" asked Dr. Crazybrains with a smirk.

"Or elth there'th more thlop coming your way," said Marty. He was holding a fistful of "food" ready to launch at the doctor.

"You really think a little food can stop me, kid?" asked Dr. Crazybrains, walking toward him. As Marty started to throw his "food," the Igloo-Goo's effects spread down his arm. It flash-froze and skewed his aim.

The "food" fastball whizzed past the doctor's head. It splattered right in front of the school principal as he walked through the cafeteria. He slipped on the "food" and fell backward onto table #12 (the table for kids obsessed with the monster card game Chi-Chi-Mookipon).

The principal crashed into a pile of gross half-eaten sandwiches, sticky juice boxes, and some very valuable, ultra-rare collectible cards. He was buried under the mess, and all the kids in the cafeteria burst out laughing.

A lightbulb went off in Skyler's head. A little food wouldn't stop Dr. Crazybrains, but a lot of food could. She yelled at the top of her lungs . . .

The battle cry set off a lunchroom riot. Every kid went crazy. This wasn't a food fight—this was a food *war*. The doctor was hit with the full menu: milk carton missiles to the front, orange-slice torpedoes to the back, tuna salad bombs to the gut. It was a full assault of salt and pepper.

Skyler ran through the chaos to Marty. She pulled on his frozen arm. "We have to get you out of here, Marty! C'mon!"

But Marty didn't budge. Both his legs were now iced over. He couldn't even lift his sneaker off the ground. From his toes to his neck, the Igloo-Goo had taken over his whole body. The blue frost crept over Marty's face, and with a sin-  gle exhale of white mist, Marty was completely transformed into a frozen statue.

"He's a human icicle!" Ralph yelled.

Skyler swiped up her skateboard and tossed it onto the floor. "Ralph, help me put him on this. We can wheel him out!"

Dr. Crazybrains saw Ralph and Skyler load the Marty statue onto the skateboard. The kids pushed Marty toward the exit. The doctor tried to stop them, but he was trapped in a storm of cafeteria food.

"No! No! No!" whined the doctor. "Escaping

on a skateboard wasn't part of my plan at all! I'll have to add a bonus step." The doctor pulled out another one of his potions. "Step three and a half! I get stuck in a food fight, and I use my Blocker Brew!"

Blocker Brew was the doctor's super-shield formula. Dr. Crazybrains gulped down the potion. A glowing force field appeared around his body. It blocked all the flying food. Nothing got through the shield. Dr. Crazybrains now had a clear path to grab Marty.

Just as Skyler and Ralph wheeled the Marty statue to the doorway, the doctor jumped in front of them. "Not so fast!" exclaimed Dr. Crazybrains. "I'm taking your friend to my mansion's underground lab!"

He pulled out a bottle of Trip Sip. It was a warp potion that teleported you anywhere in the world.

"So sorry, but this dosage is only for two," the doctor said. He poured it over himself and Marty.

In a **POOF!** of purple smoke, they were gone.

CHAPTER 17

The Mom Problem

THE FOOD FIGHT was such a sloppy mess that the principal canceled school for the rest of the afternoon. Skyler and Ralph decided they'd meet back at Marty's house, get Awesome Dog, jet to the secret lab, and stop Dr. Crazybrains.

There was one problem with this plan: Marty's mom.

Let's put your imagination to the test (don't worry—this test doesn't require a number-two pencil or anything):

Skyler and Ralph must retrieve Awesome Dog from inside Marty's house. The most obvious solution is to knock on the front door and calmly explain to Mrs. Fontana that an evil scientist with an arsenal of superpowered potions has taken her son, and the only chance of saving him is to use the high-tech flying robot dog parked in his bedroom.

Which one of the following possibilities do you think has the best result?

OPTION A

Hearing this information about revenge, weird science, and a robotic pet causes Mrs. Fontana's brain to short-circuit with mom panic overload. She suffers temporary memory loss and forgets which kitchen drawer holds the spoons.
End result: Dr. Crazybrains still gets his revenge, and Mrs. Fontana tragically eats cereal with a fork for an entire week.

OPTION B

Hearing this information about revenge, weird science, and a robotic pet causes Mrs. Fontana to call the police. The cops discover the secret laboratory, but Dr. Crazybrains uses a potion to transform the entire police force into goldfish.

End result: Dr. Crazybrains still gets his revenge, and the police headquarters is turned into a giant aquarium.

OPTION C

Hearing this overwhelming information about revenge, weird science, and a robotic pet causes Mrs. Fontana to immediately get Awesome Dog and find Dr. Crazybrains herself. However, having never piloted a robot dog before, she mistakenly flies past the lab, rockets off ten thousand miles away, and crash-lands at the North Pole. **End result:** Dr. Crazybrains still gets his revenge, and Mrs. Fontana is chased by a polar bear.

The only option that doesn't end horribly is **Option D:** none of the above. This was the safest strategy. Skyler and Ralph would have to sneak inside Marty's house and get Awesome Dog undetected, without Mrs. Fontana ever finding out.

It would be a very top-secret operation.

CHAPTER 18

A Very Top-Secret Operation

SKYLER SKATEBOARDED as fast as she could to Marty's house. When she rolled up to the front yard, she saw Marty's mom through the living room window. Skyler quickly dove behind the bushes to avoid being spotted. She noticed the bush next to her was wearing square glasses.

Suddenly, the shrub said, "Fun fact! An octopus can camouflage itself by—"

"AH!" yelled Skyler. She swung her skateboard into the talking bush like a broadsword.

"OW! Hey! It's just me, Ralph, in a bush costume." He pulled off the leafy disguise. "I figured if we're sneaking into Marty's bedroom, we'd need some equipment. I stopped by the All-Mart superstore. My nana gave me a gift card last Christmas."

From his backpack, Ralph laid out all his new gear. Not only had he purchased a shrub suit, but he also had a toolbox, a grappling hook, nightvision googles, suction-cup gloves, smoke bombs, and a candy bar.

All-Mart sold everything.

"And what exactly are we supposed to do with this stuff?" asked Skyler.

"I got it all worked out," said Ralph, eating the candy bar. "We disconnect the house's security alarm, crawl through the air-conditioning vents, lasso Awesome Dog, throw smoke bombs at Mrs. Fontana, and disappear in the confusion. We can call our mission either Operation: Fontana House Phantoms or Operation: Hush Puppy. Which do you think is better, Skyler? . . . Skyler?"

Ralph was so focused on laying out his strategy he didn't realize Skyler had left already. She wasn't going to waste time playing spy games. She'd used her daredevil skills to shimmy up the drainpipe and was now crawling in through Marty's bedroom window.

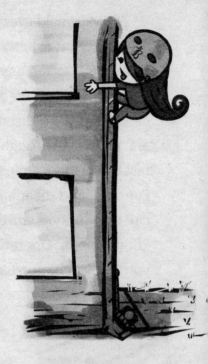

"Skyler?! Wait up! SKYLER!" Ralph yelled from below. He grabbed hold of the drainpipe to try to follow her, when—

"Ralph? What are you doing out here?" asked Mrs. Fontana. She had heard the screaming and had come outside.

"Oh. Hi! Mrs. Fontana. I'm just . . ." Ralph needed a good cover story fast. He looked to his gear and said, "Just going door to door selling spy equipment for our school fundraiser. We're taking a field trip to . . . Japan to visit a ninja museum."

This was a terrible cover story.

"Mrs. Fontana, can I interest you in a set of night-vision goggles?" asked Ralph with an awkward smile.

CHAPTER 19

‖‖

House Hunting

‖‖

IN MARTY'S BEDROOM, Skyler found Awesome Dog powered down in the corner. She flipped his on switch. The dog sparked to life.

"We need your help, Awesome Dog," said Skyler. "Marty's in trouble and—"

"BARK. BARK. PROTECTING MARTY. ACTIVATING MEGA-CANNON," said Awesome Dog. His bazooka popped out of his back.

"Whoa, whoa, whoa! Easy there. Marty's not here. That's the problem," Skyler said. She pushed the mega-cannon down into its chamber. "An evil scientist has Marty in an underground lab. Do you remember the address of that mansion you and Marty crashed?"

"BARK. BARK. SCANNING FOR EVIL SCIENTIST'S MANSION," said Awesome Dog. His eyes turned into submarine-style radar screens. His ears opened into two rotating satellite dishes. His GPS began searching every street in the city.

"SCANNING. SCANNING. SCANNING," said Awesome Dog.

Down in the front yard, Mrs. Fontana donated five dollars to Ralph's made-up ninja fundraiser. When she went back inside the house, she heard a robot voice coming from her son's bedroom. She called up, "Marty? Is that you?"

Skyler panicked. She couldn't let Mrs. Fontana catch them. They had to find the mansion immediately. Skyler grabbed Awesome Dog by his satellite ears and twisted them faster. It sped up the search but also rushed his speech.

He blurted out, `"SCAN-SCAN-SCAN-SCAN-SCAN-SCAN-SCAN-SCAN."`

A robot repeatedly yelling "scan" made Mrs. Fontana realize something was wrong. She went up the stairs to investigate. Skyler heard Mrs. Fontana getting closer with every creaking step.

`"SCAN-SCAN-SCAN-SC—MANSION LOCATED!"` Awesome Dog said.

Mrs. Fontana opened Marty's bedroom door to find—

The room covered in broken glass and splintered wood chips. Skyler and Awesome Dog were gone.

Luckily, they'd flown out of the bedroom milliseconds earlier. Unluckily, there hadn't been time to open the bedroom window first.

"This is insanity!" Mrs. Fontana yelled, throwing her arms in the air. "What is going on with this new house! First the TV remote doesn't work, then the front yard catches fire, and now a window mysteriously explodes!"

Skyler and Awesome Dog jetted from the house, picked up Ralph, and rocketed toward the mansion to battle Dr. Crazybrains.

CHAPTER 20

Mayor Sweetcheeks of Fancy Town

FLOATING HIGH IN THE SKY among the bubble-gum clouds was a magical place called Fancy Town. Fancy Town had rainbow streets lined with beautiful cupcake houses. Everyone who lived there was super nice, and everything had a sparkly shine.

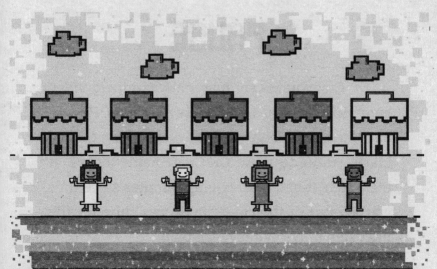

One day, Mayor Sweetcheeks had a tea party and invited his dearest friend, Princess Snuggle-wuggles. They sat in fluffy pink chairs, sipped yummy glittery tea, and had a very polite talk about cuddly kitty cats—

PAUSE

Dr. Crazybrains set down his handheld video game *Sparkle Rainbow Tea Party Adventure*. He was back in his underground lab waiting for the icy Marty statue to thaw. Dr. Crazybrains looked at his watch. It had been twenty minutes since they warped out of the cafeteria. It was time for the next step in his evil revenge plan.

Dr. Crazybrains tucked his game system into his limited-edition *Sparkle Rainbow Tea Party Adventure* smiley-cupcake fanny pack and checked on his new prisoner.

Marty was locked in one of the empty banana beast cages. The Igloo-Goo had finally melted, leaving Marty drenched in ice water. His spiked hair was wet and fell flat against his head. He was shivering from the cold.

Dr. Crazybrains peeked into the cage and teased, "Hey, kid! What are you doing? Just *chilling* out?" The doctor gave a big evil laugh at his own joke.

Marty didn't think it was funny at all. He was freezing and wanted out of the cage and into warm, dry socks. He pleaded with Dr. Crazybrains. "Look, I feel really bad for crashing your mansion, but can't you just use one of your potions to fix it?"

"You're right. I could use my Fixer Elixir. It's a potion that repairs anything," the doctor said. He pointed to a small bottle on his shelf. The bottle's label showed a screwdriver and gear. "But first I was thinking of using a potion that . . . TRANS-FORMS YOUR FEET INTO LUMPS OF SPAGHETTI!!!"

The doctor dramatically pointed at another potion. This bottle had an image of a man standing in noodles.

Marty was shocked. "You're horrible! How can anyone be so evil?"

The doctor flashed an insane grin. He had

been waiting for Marty to ask him that very question. He said, "Congratulations! You've made it to step six of my perfect evil revenge plan! This is the part where I tell you the amazing backstory of how I became a supervillain. I also did some cool drawings to jazz it up."

Okay. Wait . . . again. Before we go to the next chapter, there should be another warning to the reader.

BOOK WARNING! BOOK WARNING! BOOK WARNING!

If you expected Dr. Crazybrains to have some zany and goofball reason why he became a supervillain, then this backstory isn't for you. Our apologies if you were misled. Even though *Awesome Dog 5000* has been a comedy so far, this next backstory is a twisted tale of very serious evil.[*]

---

[*] Serious evil includes delicious ice cream, family fun, and a business card. If you're not afraid of these items, then you should be okay to proceed.[**]

[**] If these things do scare you, have an adult read the chapter to you instead. Unless they get scared easily, too. In that case, maybe just jump ahead to chapter 22.

CHAPTER 21

A Twisted Tale of Serious Evil

Written by

Dr. Crazybrains

Illustrated by

Dr. Crazybrains

My journey down the path to evil began on a dark and stormy night. There was also a full moon with Halloween-style bats flying across it, and I think I heard a wolf howl in the distance.

It might have *been* a werewolf or a dude with a really, really hairy *back*. Either way, it was all very *spooky*.

It was on this night of terror that I . . .

OPENED MY OWN
ICE CREAM SHOP!

I actually should have waited until morning to open the shop, when it wasn't raining and bats weren't flying around, but I was really excited to start my new business.

 This was long before I was an evil mad scientist. Back then I was just a guy who loved making ice cream. What I enjoyed most was creating original flavors. It was my dream to make the world smile when people tasted my delicious new flavors.

I crafted thousands of unique and fun recipes like pepperoni pizza; "so good, you forget math" chocolate-caramel flavor; and my all-time silliest flavor: orange sherbet.

 But no one wanted any of them.

Day after day, I watched people walk past my shop in disgust. They would stand at the store window and stick their tongues out at me. Some walked inside, gave me a thumbs-down, and then said, "I'm writing a bad review on the internet about you!" One guy even bought an ice cream sundae just so he could immediately stomp

on it. I never understood why the entire neighborhood hated my fun flavors.

Everything changed, though, when a tall man in a black cape with a mechanical claw hand came to my shop. He was with his two kids, who also had black capes and claw hands. They were having a family day together and stopped in for a tasty treat.

What happened to all of their hands? Where did they get matching capes? Most importantly, why am I asking all

these questions? I don't know! It's not important! This chapter's about my amazing backstory, not the claw-hand family's fashion choices!

Mr. Clawhand asked me to create him a new flavor. He wanted the most evil ice cream ever made. It was an odd request. I had never created anything evil before, but I wasn't going to waste the chance for someone to finally try my unique flavors.

I immediately whipped together some ingredients: squid ink, snake venom, tarantula hair, and mint chocolate chip. I threw it all in a blender and served it on three sugar cones.

The family took one lick of their evil ice cream and scrunched up their faces. They didn't smile. They were disgusted. The daughter shrieked, "Daddy! It's awful!"

Her father's claw hand snapped onto my collar. He pulled me in close. I was terrified as he slowly reached under his cape with his normal hand and pulled out . . .

A BUSINESS CARD!

Mr. Clawhand wasn't just some regular father with a black cape and a mechanical claw. He was the president of the League of World Supervillains and Other Mean People. He explained to me that I had unknowingly opened my new ice cream shop next door to his international headquarters. That is why no one wanted my nice flavors. Everyone in the neighborhood was a supervillain who only liked the taste of evil.

Mr. Clawhand made me a business offer, but it wasn't for my ice cream. He wanted to use my superior mixing skills to create evil potions. I then could sell them to all the super-villains in the league. Mr. Clawhand told me that with his help I could become the world's *coolest* new supervillain!

He put his pincer around my shoulder and said, "Listen, buddy. You don't have to give up your dream. A frown is just an upside-down smile. You'll still be making people happy. They'll just all be villains. Like you."

This was a once-in-a-lifetime opportunity. I could finally stop all the teasing and mean insults and get people to accept me. All I had to do was change everything about myself and become evil.

The choice was easy. Who didn't want to be cool? I decided that day I would no longer be Ned the Nice Ice Cream Guy. I would forever be . . .

I signed Mr. Clawhand's contract and created my first potion. I then made the guy who stomped on my ice cream drink it. His head was transformed into a giant toilet. Now everyone calls him T. P. McFlush-face, and all us supervillains make fun of him.

T.P. McFLUSH-FACE

THE END

Marty sat in his cage patiently listening to Dr. Crazybrains's backstory. After it was over, the doctor gave a big, wild-eyed smile and asked, "Pretty amazing, right? What'd you think of my sweet drawings?"

Marty was confused. "Wait. The reason you became a supervillain was because some bad guy in a cape gave you a business card? That backstory wasn't amazing at all. The whole thing took place in an ice cream shop."

"Yeah. I know. I know. I was going to include a lot more stuff," Dr. Crazybrains explained, "but my hand got tired from drawing all the pictures, so I shortened the backstory. I left out how I fell into toxic sludge and it gave me super-intelligence, and how I met my butler on an adventure in Australia. I also fought three cobras to get venom for that evil ice cream recipe."

"That stuff is totally amazing. You should definitely include that stuff in your story next time," Marty said.

"WELL, TOO BAD! There won't be a next time for you!" screamed Dr. Crazybrains. "Your time is up, you spike-haired pipsqueak! We're now on step seven! This is when I choose a final potion and complete my perfect evil revenge!"

CHAPTER 22

<hr>

From Zeroes to Heroes

<hr>

DR. CRAZYBRAINS went to his wall of a thousand potions to decide which one to use on Marty. The doctor narrowed his choices down to two potions.

One bottle's label showed a rabbit. "I could use my Cutie-Pie Potion on you," the doctor said. "This will transform you into an adorable little bunny. Then I'll sell you to a grandma who will name you Fluffikins and give you wet, slobbery smooches every day on your cheeks!"

Marty couldn't imagine living as a rabbit. He hated eating carrots and really hated gross grandma kisses.

Dr. Crazybrains held up the second potion. This label showed two large half circles. "Or I could use my Tons-of-Tush Tonic? It makes your butt

twenty times bigger. You'll never walk through a door again!" said the doctor.

Marty gasped. Where would he ever find underwear that big?

The doctor made his decision. He grabbed both potions and said, "I choose—"

But his decision was interrupted. Awesome Dog, Ralph, and Skyler crashed into the lab.

"Zeroes Club in the house—or rather, in the mansion! Woop-woop!" yelled Ralph.

The explosion from their entrance sent Dr. Crazybrains flying. His potions flipped into the air, and he belly-flopped into a potion-mixing vat.

Dr. Crazybrains was defeated.

Awesome Dog and the kids flew to Marty's cage. They didn't need a key. Awesome Dog used the thruster fire from his rocket paw to melt the lock off. Marty was finally freed.

"You came just in time!" said Marty. He was so relieved to be saved. Marty gave Skyler and Ralph high fives. "Thanks for rescuing me, and thanks for defeating Dr. Crazybrains, Awesome Dog!"

CO-OP MODE

"BARK. BARK. TOO EASY," said Awesome Dog.

But Awesome Dog's work wasn't done yet. A monstrous roar boomed out, "YOU RUINED MY BIRTHDAY! THEN YOU RUINED MY REVENGE PLAN! NOW I'M GOING TO DO A RE-REVENGE PLAN!"

A shadowy figure lifted its head out of the potion-mixing vat.

CHAPTER 23

The Re-revenge Plan

WHEN DR. CRAZYBRAINS fell into the mixing vat, his revenge potions came with him. The Cutie-Pie Potion and the Tons-of-Tush Tonic mixed into an awful combination. It created a hideous monster covered in soft white fur. It had a pink twitchy nose and two fluffy ears sprouting from its bald head. It was Dr. Crazybrains, but he was transformed into a little bunny . . .

WITH TWENTY-FOOT-TALL BUTT CHEEKS!!!

"YOU DON'T MIND IF I *BUTT* IN, DO YOU?" asked Dr. Crazybunny.

The doctor hammered his enormous butt cheeks down toward Marty, Ralph, and Skyler. The kids jumped aside, barely dodging the attack. The doctor missed and shattered his experiment table. All the banana beasts scattered across the lab.

"We need to get out of here fast," said Marty. All three kids grabbed on to Awesome Dog's leash. Marty ordered, "Let's jet, Awesome Dog!"

Awesome Dog's rocket paws fired up. It was blastoff in three . . . two . . . one—

"BARK. BARK. OUT OF BATTERY POWER," said Awesome Dog.

The dog's thrusters sputtered out. He flopped over sideways. His eye lights went dark.

"Un-fun fact," Ralph said. "Double-A batteries only last two days in a robot dog."

Dr. Crazybunny cackled with evil laughter. The kids needed a getaway plan, or they were going to be smooshed by a massive bunny butt.

"If we can't run, we'll have to stand up to him. Boss battle–style," said Skyler.

"Boss battle? Are you insane?!" said Ralph. "How do you expect three fifth graders to take on a giant doctor-bunny thing? We don't have any weapons or karate moves, and fart codes don't work in real life!"

Marty looked around the room for anything that could help them. He then got a crazy idea.

"Maybe there is a cheat code for this. How about up, up, down, down, B, A, select . . . a potion?"

Skyler understood Marty's plan. She nodded. "Aw, yeah! Time for a power-up!"

"Let's use the doctor's potions against him," Marty said with a smirk.

CHAPTER 24

Boss Battle

THERE WERE ONLY a few seconds to search the wall of potions before the doctor was in butt-striking range. The kids needed to find the perfect potion to stop his superpowered butt cheeks from crushing them. Unfortunately, none of the bottle labels had any words, only pictures.

"How are we supposed to know which one to

pick if we don't know what any of them do?" said Ralph.

"Just guess!" said Marty.

"But choose something that looks powerful!" said Skyler.

The kids randomly picked six potions, one for each hand. Skyler turned and faced the doctor first. She held up her potion. "Back off or you'll be splashed with—with—" She didn't know what was in the bottle. The label had a scary skull and cross-bones, so she guessed. "With this poison potion!"

Dr. Crazybunny didn't show any signs of fear. He wiggled his butt and prepared to attack. Skyler threw the potion at the doctor and hoped it would work.

The potion hit Dr. Crazybunny square in the chest. A thick black goo dripped down his front and soaked into his fur. The potion's effect was strong, but not how Skyler expected.

First, an eye patch grew over the doctor's left bunny eye. Then Dr. Crazybunny's paw mutated into a hook. One of his teeth turned gold, and a treasure map tattoo appeared across his giant left butt cheek.

Dr. Crazybunny's voice turned gruff. "Sorry, lass. That thar skull-and-crossbones label don't mean poison! Ye just used one of me favorite potions—it's called Pirate Punch! ARG! I'm going ta cut ye landlubbers ta ribbons!"

He wasn't Dr. Crazybunny anymore. Now he was . . .

DR. PIRATE-CRAZYBUNNY!!!

It was Ralph's turn to attack. His potion was filled with a shiny, clear liquid. The label had a circle with exploding lines.

"Bombs away!" said Ralph, thinking it was an explosion potion. Ralph took a step to throw, but his foot slipped on an escaped banana beast. It caused him to drop the bottle, which broke across the floor.

"Watch yer step!" said Dr. Pirate-Crazybunny with a smile. "That wasn't no bomb potion, matey! Ye just swabbed the deck with me Bubble-Trouble Potion."

The spill began foaming into a massive blob of soap suds, and one tiny bubble emerged. At first, it was a normal-sized bubble like you'd see in the bathtub, but it kept growing and growing until it was the size of a car.

"Let's set sail!" said the doctor. He waved his butt cheeks up and down, fanning the bubble toward Ralph. It engulfed his whole body and trapped him inside.

Ralph was helpless as the bubble carried him into the air.

Ralph calmly said, "Fun fact! Ebulliophobia is the fear of bubbles!" Then he realized he was ten feet off the ground and yelled out, "Bonus fun fact: I cannot spell 'ebulliophobia,' but I definitely have it!!!"

Dr. Pirate-Crazybunny jumped up. He popped the bubble with his hook and grabbed Ralph by his hoodie.

Marty had to act quickly to save Ralph. He would have to decide which of his potions to use next. His right hand held a bottle labeled with fingers shocked by lightning bolts. His other potion's label showed a face with crossed-out eyes.

"Prepare to get zapped!" Marty said. He threw the potion with the lightning bolts.

The potion hit the pirate-bunny in the head, and he dropped Ralph. Ralph ran back to Marty. They watched as the doctor's body twitched and glowed blue. It looked incredibly painful, but then a smile crept across Dr. Pirate-Crazybunny's face. He said, "Ye ain't too savvy at picking potions. The label don't mean it'll electrocute someone who touches it," said the doctor. "It's me Lightning-Hand Elixir! It makes ye shoot electricity from yer fingertips. I'm

going ta fry ye to a crisp—THEN I'm going ta cut ye ta ribbons!"

Marty made the wrong choice, and now they faced a Dr. Electro-Pirate-Crazybunny.

The doctor aimed his glowing paw back at the kids. A giant lightning bolt shot out. They dove behind Awesome Dog as a white-hot blast of electricity missed them and hit Awesome Dog's belly. They weren't hurt, but the doctor was charging up his paw for another attack.

"What'd we do? Every time we try to stop the doctor, we just end up making him more dangerous," said Ralph.

"Don't worry, guys. I got this," said Skyler. "My last potion has a fireball on the label. It has to work." She threw it at Dr. Electro-Pirate-Crazybunny.

It struck him square in his pink nose and splashed across his face. The doctor's eye welled up with tears. It looked like he was going to cry. He wailed, "Ugh. I can't believe ye did that! ARRRRRG! IT HURTS SO BAD!"

"Yes!" said Skyler. "You messed with the wrong fifth graders, and now my potion is going to make you burst into flames or melt or . . . something else bad involving fire!"

"What? No! That weren't no potion, ya scally-wag! It was just a bottle of hot sauce," said Dr. Electro-Pirate-Crazybunny. "I put it on me tacos. I keep the bottle on me potion shelf when I have lunch in the lab."

Dr. Electro-Pirate-Crazybunny was now furious. He was done messing around. He wiped the hot sauce from his eye and did a giant bunny hop. He landed right next to the kids. The doctor towered over them and raised his lightning paw. It glowed a bright neon blue, fully charged for a second blast. Marty, Skyler, and Ralph were about to be burnt toast.

"Any last words?" asked the doctor.

"BARK. BARK. BATTERIES RECHARGED!" a voice answered.

It was Awesome Dog. His eyes were lit up bright yellow. The doctor's previous lightning attack had missed the kids, but it had jolted Awesome Dog's batteries back to life.

And the electro-pirate-bunny-doctor was shaking in his evil fur.

FULL POWER

CHAPTER 25

Full Power

AWESOME DOG WAS RECHARGED, and his eyes were locked onto his target, Dr. Electro-Pirate-Crazybunny.

The doctor put his hands up in the air and pleaded, "Uh, nice doggy?"

TARGET ACQUIRED
DR. ELECTRO-PIRATE-CRAZYBUNNY
FEAR LEVEL: MAXIMUM SCARED

SCANNING POSSIBLE ATTACKS:

RANGE : 87 FT. 8 IN.

76293286
29726574
83726294
99047791
88925881
94828987
66169850

GIANT BUTT HAMMER
EVIL POTIONS
ELECTRO-ZAPS
PIRATE STARS
CUTE BUNNY NOSE TWITCHES
WEIRD EYEBROWS

63.2% THREAT: HOOK

84.7% THREAT: LIGHTNING PAW

1.8% THREAT: SILLY BEARD

A.D.S.K. VISION

"Hey, Dr. Crazybrains. Check this out." Marty tossed over his remaining potion. It was an easy catch for the bunny.

"You wanna know what this p-p-potion does?" stuttered the terrified doctor.

"Oh, I don't really care what special power the potion has," said Marty. He smiled. "Awesome Dog just likes to play fetch. Get that potion, boy."

Dr. Electro-Pirate-Crazybunny looked to the bottle in his paw. He gasped. He knew exactly what was about to happen.

"BARK. BARK. ACTIVATE MEGA-CANNON!" said Awesome Dog.

Awesome Dog's giant bazooka extended out of his back. He targeted the potion bottle and fired.

Dr. Electro-Pirate-Crazybunny was blasted through the wall and sent screaming into the clouds. After a few seconds, he was the size of a little dot, then a speck, and then he was gone completely.

"BARK. BARK. TARGET HAS BEEN SENT TO JUPITER!" said Awesome Dog.

The next day, Awesome Dog earned a medal for bravery from the president. Marty became the

most popular kid in school. Skyler set a world record in skateboarding. And Ralph won a million dollars on the *Fun Fact Trivia Show*. They all lived happily ever after. What a nice, sweet ending—

Oh, wait a second. That's not how this story ends at all. This is what really happened:

Right after Dr. Crazybrains was sent to Jupiter, Mr. Poopsie entered the lab. "Pardon the interruption, children. I was instructed by Master Crazybrains that in the event of his defeat, I'm to destroy his mansion and escape with all his potions."

The butler scooped up all the doctor's potions into a Santa-sized bag. From his butler jacket, he pulled out a remote and clicked its big red button.

"Toodles," said Mr. Poopsie. He poured a warp potion on himself and disappeared.

A loud alarm sounded: "WARNING! WARN-
ING! SELF-DESTRUCT COUNTDOWN STARTING!
THE MANSION WILL EXPLODE IN TEN SECONDS!"

CHAPTER 26

Escape from the Mansion

THE MANSION'S SELF-DESTRUCT program started. The lab walls rumbled. The floor and walls cracked. The kids had to escape the underground laboratory before it was too late. A speaker counted down until total destruction.

"I think it's time we take Awesome Dog on that walk now!" said Skyler.

Marty, Ralph, and Skyler grabbed the dog's leash. His rocket paws fired up, and they all jetted into the air.

The ceiling split in half, and the mansion above collapsed into the lab. Dr. Crazybrains's house and everything in it rained down.

Awesome Dog zigzagged through wave after wave of falling bricks, couches, toilets, refrigerators, and a beanbag chair collection.

Awesome Dog shielded the kids from the falling debris, taking the full force of the damage. His metal body was dented, scraped, and pummeled from all angles.

In the distance, Marty spotted a ray of sunlight shining through the dust. It was a small opening to the outside. "There! That's our exit!" he yelled.

"BARK. BARK. GOING UP," said Awesome Dog. He ramped his boosters to max power and rocketed even faster, plowing through the mansion wreckage.

Awesome Dog's damaged body rattled. Nuts and bolts fell out. One of his ears blew away. His eye lights flickered. Sections of his metal plating ripped free. Between the severe hits and the stress of the speed, Awesome Dog was being torn apart.

But he refused to slow down.

He held his rocket paws steady and pushed his rockets to the limit, and just as Awesome Dog shot out of the lab—

The mansion erupted in a gigantic explosion. It was like a grenade thrown into a pile of dynamite stacked in a bomb factory built inside a missile.

So, uh, yeah. It was a pretty big explosion.

When the smoke cleared, Marty was covered in ash. Ralph and Skyler were next to him, laid out on the mansion's front yard.

"Whew! That was close. I can't believe we all made it out safely!" said Marty.

"Not all of us," said Skyler. She was staring at something in the grass. Marty turned to see—

Awesome Dog was destroyed.

His parts were scattered across the lawn. His eye lights were dark.

Their friend was gone. He had sacrificed himself to save their lives.

"Maybe we can put him back together," Ralph suggested.

Marty shook his head. "The box didn't have any instructions."

The kids were heartbroken. There was no way they could rebuild Awesome Dog. Ralph and Skyler stood up and gave Marty a hug. That's when something fell out of Ralph's hoodie pocket.

It was Ralph's second Dr. Crazybrains's potion!

Marty swiped up the bottle and looked at the label. "Ralph, why did you choose this potion to fight Dr. Crazybrains?"

Ralph shrugged and said, "I thought it would help. It had a picture of a sword and shield."

A bright smile broke across Marty's face. Ralph didn't choose a sword-and-shield potion. The symbols were a screwdriver and gear. Dr. Crazybrains had shown Marty this exact bottle earlier in the lab.

"This is a repair-anything potion!" said Marty.

CHAPTER 27

Awesome Dog Version 2.0

THE KIDS GATHERED up all of Awesome Dog's parts into a pile. Marty uncorked the repair-anything Fixer Elixir. He looked down the bottle's neck, closed his eyes, and whispered to himself, "Please work." This potion was the kids' last and only hope of saving their friend.

Marty tipped the bottle. The thick, gooey elixir slowly poured out like cough syrup. It drizzled over Awesome Dog's broken pieces. The potion seeped into the metal shards and circuitry. Then all the pieces began to glow a bright neon green.

Instantly, the potion took effect. The pile of Awesome Dog's parts hovered over the grass. They floated into the air and swirled around the mansion yard. The parts picked up speed, circling faster and faster until they whirled into a storm.

Lightning flashed. Thunder boomed. The wind grew even stronger as it formed a powerful tornado of springs, gears, and wires.

Marty, Ralph, and Skyler grabbed on to a nearby tree to keep from being sucked into the storm. Their feet were lifted off the ground as they gripped the bark.

And then . . .

The storm faded.

Marty, Ralph, and Skyler flopped back down
to the grass. The howling wind fell to a whis-
per. The clouds parted, and standing in front
of the kids was Awesome Dog, completely
reassembled.

"Holy moon cheese! I can't believe what I'm looking at," said Marty in awe.

Ralph squinted. "What *are* we looking at?" he asked. He couldn't see anything. The storm had blown his glasses to the back of his head.

"Your potion worked, Ralph. Awesome Dog is completely repaired," said Skyler, happily shocked.

Marty ran to Awesome Dog and gave him a big hug around his neck. "I thought we'd lost you, boy."

"I gotta say, Awesome Dog, those were some sick flying skills back there. Very impressive," said Skyler.

She kissed him on his nose and rubbed the back of his neck. Awesome Dog's eyes lit up with hearts, and his antenna tail wagged.

"BARK. BARK. WOWZA. WOWZA," said Awesome Dog.

Ralph adjusted his glasses over his eyes and closely examined Awesome Dog's condition. He didn't see a hint of damage. There wasn't a speck of dirt on Awesome Dog. The repair potion had even given him a fresh paint job. "This is amazing! He's as good as new!"

Actually, Awesome Dog was better than new.

"BARK. BARK. UPGRADE COMPLETE!" Awesome Dog said. He lowered his head and showed the kids his new collar. It was made of shiny black panels. The battery slot on his belly had been replaced. "SOLAR POWER INSTALLED."

Awesome Dog could now use the sun for

electricity. He'd never run out of power again, and it would save a ton of money on batteries.

"BARK. BARK. SHOULD WE GO FOR A WALK?" asked Awesome Dog.

His leash unspooled from his collar. His rocket paws lit up, ready for flight. But the kids hesitated to pick up the leash.

After what they had just gone through, Marty, Skyler, and Ralph decided to take the long way home—on their own two feet, with Awesome Dog running alongside them.

CHAPTER 28

The Next Day at School

THE NEXT DAY, Awesome Dog didn't get a medal, Skyler didn't set any world records, and Ralph didn't win a million dollars, but Marty did have a shot at being friends with the cool kids.

Marty was in the cafeteria with his tray of "food" when Shades yelled out, "Yo! New kid! Just where do you think you're going?"

Marty stopped in his tracks. He was terrified the cool kids were about to tease him again about his lunch. Marty didn't want any trouble, so he said, "Uh, I'm just going to sit far away from you and your friends and eat my puke food."

"I saw you trip the principal yesterday. It started that food fight," said Shades.

"Oh, no. That was a mistake," said Marty. He tried to apologize, but Shades didn't want to hear it.

"And it was legendary! Plus, there's a rumor going around that you've got your very own super-villain. You're pretty cool, new kid. You belong at table number one."

Marty was thrilled to get an invitation to the cafeteria's top-ranked table, but he wasn't sure he wanted to accept it. Ralph and Skyler were waiting for him at table 0.

"What about my friends Ralph Rogers and Skyler Kwon? Can they sit with us?" Marty asked.

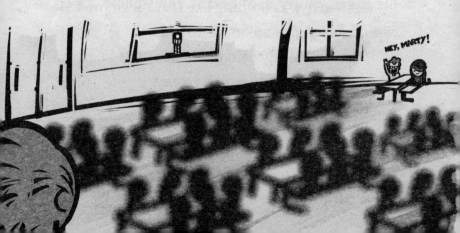

HEY, MARTY!

"What?! No way!" said Shades. "Ralph is weird. He's always yammering on about those stupid fun facts. And Skyler is an ultra-freako. Have you seen the way she dresses or listened to any of her strange music? You're one of the cool kids now, Marty. You shouldn't hang out with losers. It's called table zero because they're nobodies."

Marty thought about what it might be like to be cool. He'd never have to worry about being called a dork again, and the entire school would like him. It was an easy decision. Being a cool kid was everything Marty wanted—or was it?

The choice reminded him of Dr. Crazybrains and his epic backstory. The doctor was also given a once-in-a-lifetime chance to be popular. All he had to do was accept Mr. Claw Hand's offer and turn his back on the things he cared about.

But Marty was nothing like Dr. Crazybrains. He would never give up on his friends.

"Thanks," Marty said to Shades, "but I'll pass."

Marty turned and walked away.

Shades was so shocked, his sunglasses popped off his face. No one in school history had ever said no to the cool kids' table. But Marty didn't care. He wasn't going to ditch his friends because some lame kid in sunglasses told him to. He didn't need Shades, or a cool kids' table, or anybody who would tell him how to act or who he could hang out with. Marty's mom was right (as moms usually are)—he just needed to be himself.

Marty pulled his not-to-do list from his pocket. He took one last look at it, then crumpled it into a ball. He did a jump shot and threw it into the trash.

He joined Ralph and Skyler at the wobbly three-legged table in the corner of the cafeteria.

Marty smiled as he realized that maybe the 0 on their table wasn't just a number. It represented a circle: a circle of friends.

And that truly was everything he'd always wanted.

He announced to the table, "Today's official meeting of the Zeroes Club is now in session!"

CHAPTER 29

Doghouse Secrets

AFTER SCHOOL, the Zeroes Club went to Marty's house to play with Awesome Dog. They found him in the backyard. His head was just inside a red doghouse. His back end was hanging out with his antenna tail wagging. He was barking at something inside the doghouse, but they couldn't see what it was.

"Maybe he caught a robot squirrel," joked Skyler.

The kids crawled into the doghouse to see what had Awesome Dog's attention.

But the doghouse was empty. There were just a few old newspapers covering the floor. Marty picked one up and read the front-page story.

Marty instantly recognized the man in the picture. "This is the toothbrush-inventor guy who used to own my house. He's the guy who made Awesome Dog," said Marty. He read the first lines of the newspaper story. "It says here he disappeared ten years ago under mysterious circumstances and was never seen again."

"Check it out," said Ralph. Under the newspaper, there was a numbered keypad with a little red dot light. "It's some kind of lock. It requires a four-digit code."

Marty looked to Awesome Dog, then said, "I have a pretty good guess what the four numbers are." He typed in 5-0-0-0. The keypad flipped open to reveal a glowing green button underneath it. "What do you think it does?" Marty asked.

"Only one way to find out," said Skyler. She slapped the button with the palm of her hand. A steel plate dropped over the doorway, locking the kids inside. Then a loud thud was heard in the walls, and the doghouse floor lowered. The entire doghouse was actually a secret elevator. It was going down.

The doghouse elevator came to a stop in a small underground room with a wall of televisions.

"Whoa! Can you imagine playing *Sheriff Turbo-Karate* on this thing!" exclaimed Ralph.

Marty wasn't thinking about video games. He was focused on the screens. Each TV was playing moments from their recent adventure. It showed them playing *Sheriff Turbo-Karate* in the living room. It showed the cafeteria food fight. It even showed their battle with the big-butt Dr. Crazy-bunny.

"Someone's been watching us this whole time?!" said Skyler in disbelief.

Marty pointed to one of the screens. "Look! They're still watching us!"

The bottom-right screen showed Marty, Ralph,

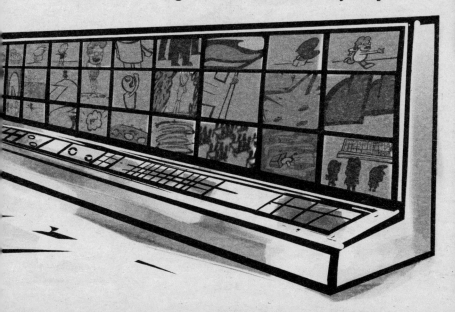

and Skyler looking at the wall of TVs. They were being recorded right now.

The kids spun around and were shocked to see an odd little machine with a propeller on its head, two metal squid arms, and a single camera lens for an eye.

The mysterious spybot hovered in the air, filming everything.

CHAPTER 30

One Last Thing, One First Thing

WHEN THE KIDS spotted the spybot, it let out a surprised *beep-boop* noise. Its propeller sped up, and it started to fly away.

"It's a spy-camera-helicopter-robot thingama-jig," said Ralph. "We have to get it!"

"BARK. BARK. ACTIVATE MEGA-CANNON!" said Awesome Dog.

"No, no, no! He didn't mean 'get it' like that!" Marty tried to stop the dog from firing, but it was too late. Awesome Dog shot his mega-cannon. The spybot exploded in a firework of burning scrap metal.

"Well, that's just great!" said Ralph. "Awesome Dog vaporized our only chance to figure out what this was all about."

"Maybe not," Skyler said. Something caught her eye in the charred debris. She pushed aside some smoldering gears and pulled out a large metal shard. She examined it with a scowl.

"What is it, Skyler?" asked Marty.

Skyler tilted the chunk of iron toward the boys. There was a white #30 etched across the side. "This has to mean something, right?" asked Skyler.

"Number thirty? Maybe he sits at an even worse table than us," joked Marty.

"Or he's on a robot football team?" guessed Ralph.

Behind Ralph, Marty noticed the wall of televisions. They were stacked five across and six high. He realized something. "Wait a second. No, it's not football, Ralph, but it could be part of a team." Marty pointed to the screen at the bottom right. It was rolling static. This wasn't a joke. He said,

"If there are thirty screens and we blew up robot number thirty, that means—"

"There could be twenty-nine more spybots out there," interjected Skyler.

"Holy moon cheese," said Marty. "We need to take a closer look at these videos. We might be able to figure out what these spybots are up to."

"Or, more important, *where* these spybots are hiding," said Skyler.

Ralph said, "Fun fact! Football was invented in the year—"

Awesome Dog interrupted with a "BARK. BARK." He was staring at one of the screens—it was a clue that would set the kids on their next awesome adventure. . . .

WANT TO HELP THE ZEROES CLUB SEARCH FOR CLUES?

You can go back to the start of this story and find all the spybots secretly filming Marty, Ralph, and Skyler.

There are thirty chapters and one spybot in each of them. These robotic sneaks are experts at blending in, so you have to look carefully. Spybots might be big or small, hiding in the shadows or flying in plain sight. Here's a little hint to get you started in chapter 1: Spybots are part of the neighborhood watch!

THINK YOU CAN FIND ALL THIRTY SPYBOTS?

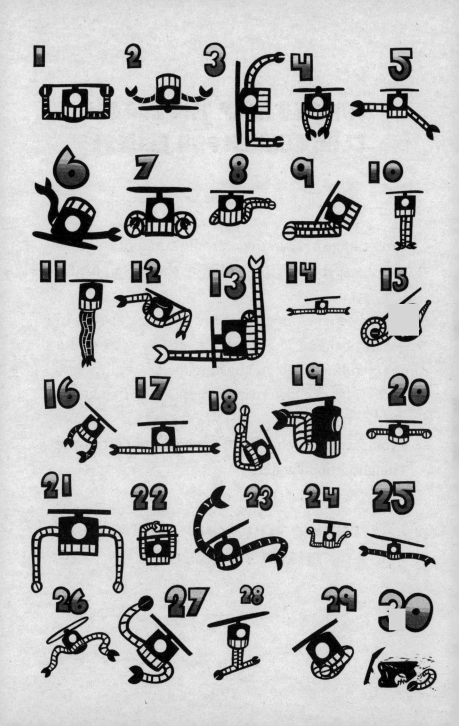

HOLY MOON CHEESE!

Awesome Dog and his pals are ready for their first real-life BOSSYPANTS battle!

Check out this sneak peek of . . .

AWESOME DOG 5000

VS. MAYOR BOSSYPANTS

JUSTIN DEAN

SPYBOT #1 ZOOMED ACROSS the city with Awesome Dog and Marty hot on its tail. Awesome Dog was fast, but the spybot was incredibly agile.

The spybot took a quick right around a big blue mailbox on the sidewalk. Awesome Dog followed but cut the turn too close. He clipped the mailbox's side. It exploded in a flurry of envelopes. Marty was trying his best to steer Awesome Dog,

but yanking on a leash isn't an accurate control system.

The spybot zigzagged between houses and across backyards. Then it hooked a sharp left down a dead-end street. When Awesome Dog rounded the corner, the spybot was nowhere to be seen.

"Hold up, Fives," said Marty. "Fives" was the new nickname the Zeroes Club had decided on for their pet. It was way better than the first nickname they had tried, "A-Doggie-Dog Five Grand."

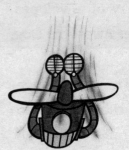

Fives powered down his thrusters and landed on the sidewalk. Just then, Ralph caught up on his scooter. He was sweating and out of breath. Keeping up with a rocket-powered dog is exhausting.

"Did you lose him?" huffed Ralph.

Marty shook his head. "That little sneak is hiding here somewhere."

The spybots were designed to camouflage themselves. They could contort their bodies to blend into any environment. There were a ton of places to hide on the dead-end street: trash cans, shrubs, garden gnomes—and one very suspicious fire hydrant.

Marty pressed his finger to his lips. He gave

Awesome Dog a "shh," then pointed at the fire hydrant. Marty whispered, "Grab that spybot, Fives."

"BARK. BARK. CAPTURING SPYBOT," said Awesome Dog.

His rocket paws ignited. He shot forward in a blur. Suddenly, the hydrant revealed its true form. The spybot's propeller popped out of the top of its head. Its arms snaked out from its sides. Awesome Dog flew in and bit onto the spybot's wrist to hold it in place. The spybot's propellers spun faster as it tried to escape. Awesome Dog clenched his jaws. The spybot slowly lifted itself—with Awesome Dog attached—off the ground.

Marty grabbed on to Awesome Dog's leash. He leaned back to try to pull the pair down, but the spybot was still gaining altitude. Then Ralph dove onto Marty's ankles. That kept the spybot from going higher, but not from moving forward. The spybot towed its three unwanted passengers across a front yard. Ralph was dragged face-first through a bed of flowers. He yelled in between spitting out petals, dirt, and leaves: "I—*pfft*—can't—*pfft*—hold—*pfft*—on—*pfft*—much—*pfft*—longer!"

CRACK! The spybot was swatted down with a heavy smack of a skateboard. Skyler had shown up just in time. The spybot wobbled through the air, puffing out smoke. It chirped a few wonky beeps and bloops before it dropped to the lawn.

"Sorry I'm late," said Skyler. "I passed that kid watching the *Sheriff Turbo-Karate 2* trailer on his phone. You're right, Ralph. That game is really going to be next level."

The Zeroes Club had caught their first spybot. It was finally time to get some answers.